For martha, who would climb to
the top of a mulberry bush
—J.C.

First published in Great Britain in 2009 by Gullane Children's Books.
First published in the United States of America in 2010 by Holiday House.
All Rights Reserved
HOLIDAY HOUSE is registered in the U.S. Patent and Trademark Office.
Printed and bound in August 2019 at Tien Wah Press, Johor Bahru, Johor, Malaysia.
www.holidayhouse.com
This Jane Cabrera's Story Time edition first published in 2019 by Holiday House Publishing, Inc.
1 3 5 7 9 10 8 6 4 2

The Library of Congress has cataloged the prior edition as follows:

Library of Congress Cataloging-in-Publication Data

Cabrera, Jane.
Here we go round the mulberry bush / by Jane Cabrera. — 1st American ed.
p. cm.
Summary: A version of the well-known song featuring animals going to school, learning, going home, and getting ready for bed.
ISBN 978-0-8234-2288-3 (hardcover)
[1. Children's songs, English—United States—Texts. 2. Songs.] 1. Title.
PZ8.3.c122He 2010
782.42164026'8—dc22

ISBN: 978-0-8234-4463-2 (hardcover)

Here We Go Round the Mulberry Bush

Jane Cabrera

HOLIDAY HOUSE  NEW YORK

This is the way we all wake up,
All wake up, all wake up.
This is the way we all wake up,
On a cold and frosty morning.

This is the way we brush our teeth,
Brush our teeth, brush our teeth.
This is the way we brush our teeth,
On a cold and frosty morning.

This is the way we all get dressed,
All get dressed, all get dressed.
This is the way we all get dressed,
On a cold and frosty morning.

This is the way we march to school,
March to school, march to school.
This is the way we march to school,
On a cold and frosty morning.

Here we go round the mulberry bush,
The mulberry bush, the mulberry bush.
Here we go round the mulberry bush,
On a cold and frosty morning.

This is the way we read and write,
Read and write, read and write.
This is the way we read and write,
On a cold and frosty afternoon.

This is the way we jump and skip,
Jump and skip, jump and skip.
This is the way we jump and skip,
On a cold and frosty afternoon.

This is the way we hop home from school,
Home from school, home from school.
This is the way we hop home from school,
On a cold and frosty afternoon.

This is the way we bounce up and down,
Up and down, up and down.
This is the way we bounce up and down,
On a cold and frosty evening.

This is the way we splash around,
Splash around, splash around.

This is the way we splash around,
On a cold and frosty evening.

This is the way we settle down,
Settle down, settle down.
This is the way we settle down,
On a cold and frosty evening.

This is the way we go to sleep,
Go to sleep, go to sleep.
This is the way we go to sleep,
On a cold and frosty evening.

Good night!